1.99

Printed in the United States of America

First Edition
5 7 9 10 8 6 4

An African American
Picture Book Collection

The

JUMP AT THE SUN

TREASURY

Jump at the Sun
Hyperion Books for Children
New York

contents

These Hands

By Hope Lynne Price · Illustrated by Bryan Collier

These hands
can touch.
These hands
can feel.
These hands
create.
These hands
can build.

These hands
can reach.
Can stretch.
Can teach.

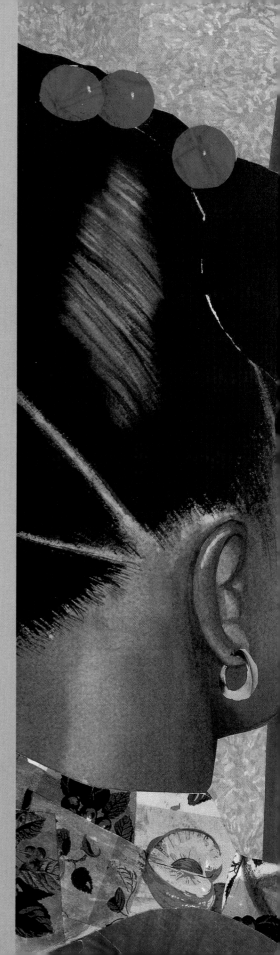

These hands
can hug.
Can pat.
Can tug.

These hands
can squeeze.
Can tickle.
Can please.

These hands can hide something inside.

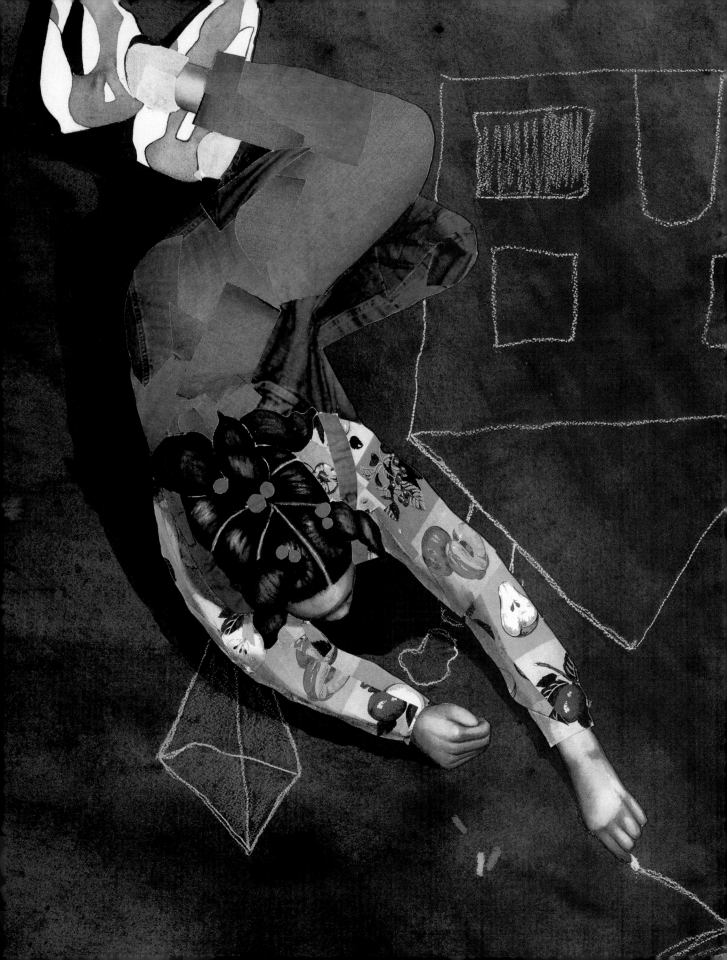

These hands
can write.
Can fly a kite.

These hands
can talk.
Help Grandma
walk.

These hands
can read.
Can share.
Can feed.

These hands
can shake
you wide
awake.

These hands
can pray.
Can clap.
Can play.

Can sow the
seeds
for a brighter
day.

Can I Pray with My Eyes Open?

By Susan Taylor Brown · Illustrated by Garin Baker

I wondered how and when and where
was the perfect way to say a prayer.

Must every prayer
be one that's spoken?
And can I pray
with my eyes open?

When I go swimming in the creek,
or play a game of hide-and-seek,

Or even when I climb a tree,
if I'm outside, can You hear me?

When I'm under the covers, out of sight,
or listening to music or flying a kite,

When I don't know
what I should do,
is that a time
to talk to You?

If I cross my fingers or stand on my head,
or get mad and my face turns red,

When I Rollerblade or ride my bike,
can I pray any time I like?

If I'm skipping rope or playing ball,
or walking backward down the hall,

When building castles at the beach,
will You still be within my reach?

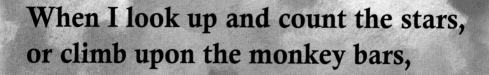

When I look up and count the stars,
or climb upon the monkey bars,

When I'm in a car, a boat, or train,
does every prayer have to be the same?

I thought it over
through and through.
Then I shared
my thoughts with You.

I got an answer right away. . . .
There's no wrong time or place to pray.

Say Hey! A Song of Willie Mays

By Peter Mandel · Illustrated by Don Tate

You were born in Alabama,
where the land lies flat.

Say hey, Willie. Say hey.

And your daddy worked the steel mill
(though he sure could swing a bat).

Say hey, Willie. Say hey.

Then you grew up not so tall,
an' there ain't no changin' that.

Say hey, Willie. Say hey.

So you played a little ball?
In the Negro Leagues was all.

Say hey, Willie. Say hey.

When the Giants sent a scout
Wasn't you they meant to call.

Say hey, Willie. Say hey.

Yeah, they signed you to a year . . .
(hope you're still here in the fall).

Say hey, Willie. Say hey.

'Cause you're nothin' but a kid
with a smooth, smooth swing.

Say hey, Willie. Say hey.

But to swing for the Giants
is a whole 'nother thing.

Say hey, Willie. Say hey.

Well, I guess you made the team.
But it's early in the spring.

Say hey, Willie. Say hey.

Hear you whiffed a steady breeze
until the crowd began to shout . . .

Say hey, Willie. Say hey.

But then, **Kaa-RACK!!**,
you smoked some singles
an' you threw some runners out. . . .

Say hey, Willie. Say hey.

Hear you're Rookie of the Year.
Man, I never had a doubt!

Say hey, Willie. Say hey.

You started sluggin' monster homers
that only you could chase. . . .

Say hey, Willie. Say hey.

You started roarin' 'round the bases
like you were in a great big race. . . .

Say hey, Willie. Say hey.

And when you drove in Giant runs
you grew a smile on your face!

Say hey, Willie. Say hey.

Say, what was that they yelled
each time you'd make the pitcher pay?

Say hey, Willie. Say hey.

Say, what was that new nickname,
which sounded better than "hooray"?

Say hey, Willie. Say hey.

Say, *what?* The *Say Hey Kid* is
what they call you to this day!

Say hey, Willie. Say hey.

Go! Go!
WILL
SAY

Now it's 1954,
and you stole the batting crown.

Say hey, Willie. Say hey.

Now you're makin' basket catches
as your cap comes flyin' down.

Say hey, Willie. Say hey.

Now you made the best grab ever.
Now you're *mayor* of this town.

Say hey, Willie. Say hey.

It doesn't matter, Willie Mays,
that you ain't no six-foot-two.

Say hey, Willie. Say hey.

It just don't matter, Willie Mays,
that I'm a poor kid just like you.

Say hey, Willie. Say hey.

It doesn't matter. You're the best.
There ain't nothin' we can't do!

Say hey, Willie. Say hey.

They say of all the sluggers
who have ever played this game . . .

Say hey, Willie. Say hey.

They say that no one ever hit
or ran or threw the same. . . .

Say hey, Willie. Say hey.

They say that you're the *greatest*
in the Baseball Hall of Fame!

Say hey.

Say Hey Facts

Nicknamed the "Say Hey Kid" because of his boyish enthusiasm, some believe Willie Mays may have been the greatest baseball player who ever lived.

Mays was a speedy center fielder for the New York Giants in the 1950s and later for the San Francisco Giants and the New York Mets. He chased down impossible fly balls and snared them, often in his famous "basket catch" with his glove at waist level. When running for the catch, his cap came flying off so frequently some people thought he wore a cap that was a couple of sizes too big—just for dramatic effect. In the 1954 World Series, Mays made what is considered the best catch of all time, grabbing a 460-foot fly ball hit by Vic Wertz of the Cleveland Indians, and whirling to throw the ball back to the infield in a single motion. This famous catch helped the Giants go on to win the series in four games.

Mays was born to a poor family in rural Alabama. While playing for the Birmingham Black Barons, a local Negro League team, he was discovered by accident when the New York Giants sent a scout to look at one of Mays's teammates. Only 5'11" and 170 pounds, Mays was still a powerful hitter. To this day, he remains in third place among baseball's greatest home run hitters (after Hank Aaron and Babe Ruth). His unique blend of base-stealing, fielding, and slugging ability has yet to be matched.

"Rogers' realistic watercolors create wonderfully expressive African American characters and a gloomy, unsettling atmosphere. . . . Children will have fun chanting along with the repeated phrases." —Booklist

A Big, Spooky House

By Donna Washington · Illustrated by Jacqueline Rogers

Author's Note

This is one of my favorite spooky stories. It has been making the rounds in the oral tradition for a very long time. I heard it for the first time almost twelve years ago as a short joke. Many people will recognize it by a number of other names—"Martin's Coming," or maybe "Pancho Villa," to name a couple. Usually, after I tell this story, a member of the audience will come up to me and announce they've heard something like it somewhere before. This is the version that I tell. I hope you will enjoy it and share it with someone else.

—D.W.

Once there was a man.

He was a **BIG** man.

He was a **STRONG** man!

And he knew it.

He went around picking fights with people just because
he knew he would win. He never walked away from trouble,
because he figured he could always battle his way out of it.

One day the people of his village told him that the army
needed volunteers.

"Since you are a big, strong man," one of the ladies told
him, "and you love to fight, you ought to see if you can
fight in the army."

He thought about that for a minute, and then he said,
"Yeah!"

He put his belongings on his back and started out down
the road.

One of his neighbors hollered after him, "Hey, it's a long walk! Do you want me to give you a ride in my cart?"

He was a **BIG** man.

He was a **STRONG** man!

He said, "I'll walk."

As he was going across the countryside, he saw an inn. The innkeeper said, "Hey, it's going to rain this evening. Why don't you stop and stay in my inn for the night?"

He was a **BIG** man.

He was a **STRONG** man!

He said, "I don't care if I get wet."

He walked until the sun went down.

As soon as the sky was dark, there was an incredible peal of thunder. *BOOM!* The skies opened, and rain fell down in sheets.

He was a **BIG** man.

He was a **STRONG** man!

He was a wet man. He didn't like it one bit.

He was looking around trying to find someplace dry,
when, in a flash of lightning, he saw a big, spooky house up
on a hill.

Now, most people would have stayed away from that
house. It was dark, and the gate was falling down. The
windows were broken and the paint was peeling. There
were holes in the roof and weeds growing all around the
yard. Most people would have stayed away, but not him.

He was a **BIG** man.
He was a **STRONG** man!
He was a not-going-to-be-
scared-by-some-spooky-house-
sitting-up-on-a-big-spooky-hill
kind of man.

He went up to the door.

When he reached out for the doorknob, the door opened all by itself. *CREAK!*

Now, most people would have left there and then. But not him.

He was a **BIG** man.

He was a **STRONG** man!

He went right in.

Outside, the place was falling apart, but inside, it was beautiful.

There was a red carpet on the floor leading down a long hallway. Even though the windows were dark outside, there were candles burning in all of the candleholders. He looked around at the beautiful, dry, warm hallway and said, "Yeah!"

He followed the red carpet to the end of the hallway. There was a huge wooden door. He reached out to open it, but it opened by itself. *CREAK!*

Now, most people might have been more than just a little frightened by this, but not him.

He was a **BIG** man.

He was a **STRONG** man!

He went right into the room.

There was a huge fire with crackling logs. There was a huge stuffed chair facing the fire. In front of the chair was a table covered with lots of good things to eat. He just looked at everything and said, "Yeah!"

Now, some people would have been too terrified to eat, but not him.

He was a **BIG** man.
He was a **STRONG** man!
He sat down and got to work.

He had that table clear in no time. When he finished, he sat back and put his feet up on a little stool. When he opened his eyes, the table had disappeared. He looked around and said, "Yeah!"

He fell asleep in front of that fire. Fast asleep in that big comfortable chair until the clock on the wall began to chime.

BONG! BONG! BONG! BONG!

It chimed twelve times. The man jumped up and said, "What! What! Oh, it's jest the clock."

The door behind him opened, and in came a black cat. Its fur was matted and dirty. Its eyes were as red as the fire. It came across the floor, scraping its claws across the wood. Its voice was thin and squeaky when it meowed. It walked over to the fireplace, jumped into the middle of the flames, picked up a flaming hot coal, and started to lick it. Then it looked straight at the man and said in a slow, screechy voice, "Are you gonna be here when John gets here?"

He was a **BIG** man.
He was a **STRONG** man!
He was a not-going-to-be-scared-by-any-cat-
sitting-in-any-fireplace-licking-any-coal kind of man.
He stared into the fireplace and said, "I'll be here when
John gets here and past that!" and he snapped his fingers
to prove he didn't care.

He sat back in his chair and went back to sleep.

BONG!

The clock struck one. The man sat up. "What! WHAT! Oh, it's jest the clock."

The door behind him opened, and in came another black cat. This one was the size of a Doberman pinscher. It had black matted fur and fiery red eyes just like the other one. Its voice was deep and snarly.

It walked over to the fireplace, sat next to the other cat, picked up a log, bit off the end, and sat there crunching noisily. It looked out at the man and said in a slow, snarly voice, "Are you gonna be here when John gets here?"

He was a **BIG** man.

He was a **STRONG** man!

He was a worried man.

But he'd never run from anything in his life, and he wasn't about to start now. So he looked straight at that great big cat and said, "I'll be here when John gets here, and past that!" Then he snapped his fingers to prove he didn't care.

He looked around at the shadows of the room, and then added, "And I'm not scared!" He sat back in that chair, and truth be told, it took him quite a while to get back to sleep.

BONG! BONG!

The clock struck two. The man sat up. "What! What! Oh, it's jest the clock."

The door behind him opened, and in came another black cat. This one was the size of a large pony. Its hair was thick and matted with straw and sticks. Its eyes were bright red, and they were so big they gave off their own light. Its voice was deep, loud, and gravelly.

It walked over to the fireplace, ate up the other two cats, licked the fireplace clean, and then turned those glowing red eyes back toward that man. It opened its mouth to show two rows of long, needle-sharp teeth. Then it said to the man in a slow, deep, gravelly voice, "Are you gonna be here when John gets here?"

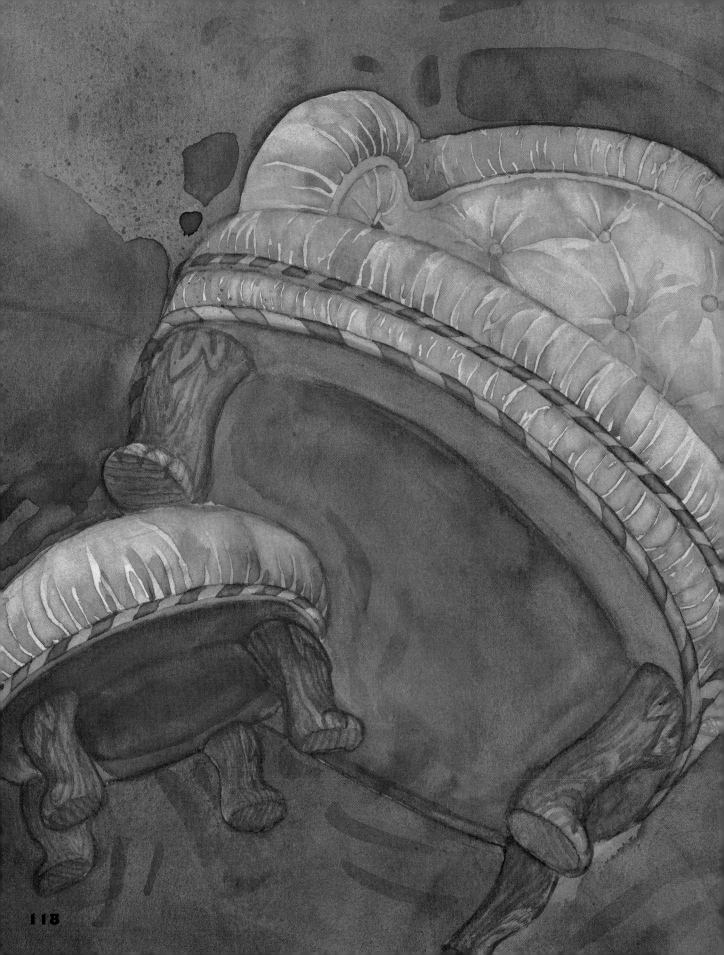

He was a **BIG** man!
He was a **STRONG** man!
He was a **GONE** man!

Granddaddy's Street Songs

By Monalisa DeGross · Illustrated by Floyd Cooper

"Granddaddy," I say, "tell me a story about long ago, when things weren't like they are today."

"I recall the summer of nineteen hundred and fifty-five," Granddaddy begins with a smile and twirls the ends of his mustache.

"Wait just one minute!" I say, stopping him so I can run and get what we need for a good, long story.

"Easy now," Granddaddy warns as I pull the blue leather photo album from the shelf and bring it to him. I slide the big book on his lap and watch as Granddaddy wipes the cover with his sleeve. I open the cover slowly, this book is so, so old.

"You can begin right here," I say and point to a picture glued on soft black paper.

"Arabbin'? You sure you want to hear about arabbin'?" Granddaddy asks, as if he thinks I've made a mistake.

"Sure do."

"Well, let me see now, where should I start?" He pretends to glance over the pictures before he begins with words that I know by heart.

"Hiii, yup! Hi, yup. Git-di-yup!" Granddaddy click-clucks his tongue to make just the right sounds. The slow toe-heel prance of Granddaddy's horse begins.

"Git it up, Daybreak, it's time to meet the mornin'!" he says. He flips his fingers and in my mind I see the reins gently slap Daybreak's broad mahogany rump.

Granddaddy makes his voice moan and groan until I can hear the wagon creak and crack, slip-slide backward just a bit, and then follow Daybreak down Central Avenue.

"Where y'all going?" I ask.

"We're on our way to the market!" Granddaddy says. "Got to load up at Camden Market."

"There's Mike Coleman standing out in front of his bicycle shop," Granddaddy points out as we head down Baltimore Street. "And right next door is Henry's Harness Shop."

"You gonna stop and say hello?" I want to know.

"Naw, not today," he says. "We got to get to the market."

As I reach over to turn the page Granddaddy says, "Whoa, slow down, Roddy. We don't want to move *too* fast." He pats my hand.

I lean toward the fuzzy black-and-white pictures. "Gee, I'll bet some of these pictures are even older than you are," I say.

"I know the buildings are," Granddaddy says with a laugh.

At the market there are rows and rows of wooden stalls. Each stall is filled with a different type of fruit or vegetable. In some pictures I see fat, funny fish resting on glassy chips of ice. I wave at the men standing beside the stalls. I like the flat straw hats on their heads and the long, shiny aprons that cover their overalls.

"Granddaddy, there are so many kinds of fruits and vegetables. How did you choose?"

"It was easy. I was careful to select only the crispest, freshest, and ripest produce for my wagon," he says proudly.

"Who is that?" I ask pointing to the next picture.

"That's Peeler!" Granddaddy says, looking pleased.

"He sure is wearing some funny-looking pants," I say, giggling.

"Roddy, that's Peeler's gimmick," he explains. "All arabbers had to have something that made them different."

"And did his gimmick work?" I ask.

"Sure did. Peeler had the second-best gimmick on the east side."

"Who had the best?" I ask with a sly smile. Granddaddy winks and moves on.

"Now look here," he says. "There's my wagon all packed and ready to go. There's a water bucket for Daybreak, and plenty of oats for him to eat. My lunch is packed in that hamper, along with my thermos filled with iced coffee. I had plenty of extra baskets—we didn't use paper bags as much as they do nowadays. And right there are my scales. I always carried two sets, and both of them were perfectly balanced."

"Now is it time to get started?" I ask, trying to rush to the next part.

"No, not yet, I got one more thing to add," he says.

"Your gimmick?" I ask, as if I don't know.

"Yes, my big fancy umbrella. It protected my produce from the hot sun. Roddy, there wasn't another umbrella like mine on the entire east side," he says, puffing up his chest.

"Or anywhere else," I add.

I look closely at the next picture, my nose nearly touching it. "That looks like me!"

"Shucks, Roddy, now you know that's not you," Granddaddy says, laughing. "You wasn't even a whisper in nineteen hundred and fifty-five. That's your daddy; he worked with me that summer. He wasn't a bit older than you are now."

"Granddaddy, he looks just like you, and I look just like him. Who do *we* all look like?"

He flips to the front of the album. And there on the first page is Great-granddaddy Slim.

"I guess all the Johnson men look alike," I say proudly, and we nod.

"Granddaddy, I wish the world was in color when you were arabbin'."

"Don't you worry, Roddy. I'm gonna describe things so well, you're gonna feel just like you were there."

"I'm ready," I say. When Granddaddy takes me on his arabbin' ride, I don't know whether to look at the pictures or him. I always try hard to do both.

Granddaddy cups his hands around his mouth and sings out:

Wa-a-a-ter-melons, I got wa-a-a-ter-melons.
Come git my wa-a-a-ter-melons.
Sweet, juicy, juicy, red to the rind.
Red, juicy, red, juicy wa-a-a-ter-melons.
Come git my wa-a-a-ter-melons.
Cantaloupe! Cantaloupe!
Honeydew! Honeydew!
Melons, melons, and melons.
I got melons, melons, and melons.

I love hearing Granddaddy's calls—they sound like songs. I begin to pat my feet to the rhythm of his voice, as he sings out loud and clear:

> *If you like what you hear*
> *Then you'll love what you see.*
> *Peaches, peaches, yes, sirree.*
> *Round, fuzzy, firm, and ripe!*
> *I'll betcha need a bib with every bite.*

All morning Granddaddy and Daybreak clip up cobblestoned streets and clop down narrow brick alleys, selling to old customers and meeting new ones as they travel along. I see babies waving, kids bouncing balls, and people laughing and talking, trying to decide just what to buy. And Granddaddy's calls help them make up their minds:

> *Ce-le-ry, long, green, and fine.*
> *If you give me a quarter, I'll give back a dime.*
> *Listen to me sing. Listen to me holler.*
> *Listen while I tell what I got for a dollar.*
> *Yellow onions—I got 'em.*
> *Summer squash—I got 'em.*
> *Got peppers, green and red.*
> *Got them hotter than you ever had.*
> *Open your doors, come out and see.*
> *Don't buy from others, just buy from me.*

When Granddaddy stops to take a deep breath, I ask, "Can I join you?"

"Roddy, you don't need to ask, just jump right in," he says, giving me a hug.

Cherries, cherries—sweet, dark cherries.
And straw-berries, straw-berries, red strawberries.
I said sweet, dark cherries and red strawberries.
Lettuce! Lettuce! Lettuce!
Let us sell you lettuce an-n-nd
Red ripe tomatoes,
Fat brown potatoes,
Sweet silver corn.
Cherries, berries, lettuce, tomatoes, potatoes, and corn.
Cherries, berries, lettuce, tomatoes, potatoes, and corn.

On and on Granddaddy and I sing and call, looking at pictures of people and places from a time long ago, before I was born. And when we see the empty wagon and there is nothing more to buy or sell, we know it's time for our last call:

We've been travelin', travelin', travelin' far,
And nothing we've sold you comes from a jar.
Our wagon is empty, there's nothing to sell.
So Daybreak and I must bid you farewell!

"Whew! That was fun," I say as we settle back on the sofa.

"Roddy," Granddaddy says, "we've been arabbin' so much, I'm just plain worn out."

I point to the last picture. "Where y'all going?" I ask.

"Shucks, I'm taking Daybreak home, he's had a long, hard day."

Granddaddy's voice is soft with memories and so is mine when I say, "So have I."

HISTORICAL NOTE

Many cities and towns in America have a tradition of street vendors selling goods and wares from horse-drawn wagons. Baltimore, Maryland, shares that tradition with one unique twist—the name by which its street vendors were known: arabbers. The origin of the name has been debated, with most scholars tracing its use to slang from nineteenth-century London, describing someone without a fixed home or place. In Baltimore, however, the terms "ay-rab" and "arabber" conjure vivid images of African-American men, selling primarily fruits, vegetables, and seafood throughout the many communities of the city. These men developed individual calls as well as special names and decorations for their horses, which were an important part of the team. They worked hard and rose early to ensure the freshness of what they were selling and to catch the attention of buyers before their fellow vendors could. Children were especially drawn to arabbers, attracted by the music and color they brought to the Baltimore neighborhoods.

Deborah Taylor
Enoch Pratt Free Library
Baltimore, Maryland

*"This effective amalgam of genres
easily draws the reader into Ailey's
life. . . . Matching the finesse of the
writing are Brian Pinkney's signature
scratchboard renderings handpainted
with oil pastels, which manage to
convey stateliness as well as
quickness, and which culminate in a
vivid, motion–filled spread featuring
dancers in Ailey's company reeling
across the stage—and seemingly
right off the pages."*
—Publishers Weekly

Alvin Ailey

By Andrea Davis Pinkney · Illustrated by Brian Pinkney

1942
True Vine Baptist Church

It seemed like the hottest day ever in Navasota, Texas, the small, dusty town where Alvin Ailey and his mother, Lula, lived. Blue-black flies buzzed their songs while the church bell rang.

Alvin and Lula worshiped at True Vine Baptist Church every Sunday. When they arrived for services, Alvin slid into his usual seat in the first-row pew. There he could watch his mother sing in the gospel choir. And Lula sure could sing. Her voice rose clear and strong as she sang the morning hymn.

The men at True Vine dressed in dignified suits. The women showed off wide-brimmed hats and fanned away the Texas heat. Some cuddled powdered babies; others hugged their Bibles.

True Vine's Reverend Lewis delivered a thundering sermon. The organ rang out, followed by a bellow of tenors singing "Rocka My Soul in the Bosom of Abraham."

Sweet sopranos and tambourines joined the rousing refrain:

Rocka-my-soul in the bosom of Abraham
Rocka-my-soul in the bosom of Abraham
Rocka-my-soul in the bosom of Abraham
Ohhh, rocka-my-soul....

The congregation made a joyful noise. They stepped and swayed with the warmth of the spirit and raised their palms in revelation. Alvin stomped his feet and clapped his hands so hard, they hurt. "Ohhh... rocka-my-soul...," he sang along.

Alvin was going to miss the music and rejoicing at True Vine Baptist Church.

Days later, Alvin rode a creaky locomotive headed west. He and Lula were going to try life in Los Angeles, California. Times had been hard in Texas; there weren't many jobs. Lula wanted a better life for Alvin. She told him there were more opportunities in the city, more ways to make a decent living.

Alvin stared out his window while the train rocked and lurched its way through the dry Texas land. Life in the city would be so different.

1945–1947
Los Angeles

Los Angeles was a flashy town. Lula found plenty of work. Most mornings she left their apartment on East 43rd Place before sunrise, and she didn't return home until the sun was long past setting.

Alvin didn't mind, though. On Saturdays and after school he liked spending time alone, exploring the city streets. He strolled Central Avenue, where nightclubs such as the Club Alabam boomed with the sounds of big-band jazz — swinging music that spilled out into the street — while the musicians inside rehearsed for the evening show.

Alvin especially liked downtown Los Angeles, where the lights on the theater houses reflected off the pavement. There was the Orpheum Theater, the Biltmore, the Rosebud, and the Lincoln.

Outside each theater a blinking marquee announced the latest show:

Pearl Bailey Performing Live
Billie Holiday — A Night of Blues
Duke Ellington and His Band

The men who owned the theaters stacked handbills on their stoops. Each handbill announced coming attractions. Alvin collected them all.

He dawdled along the sidewalk and spotted a handbill showing a black dancer, something Alvin had never seen advertised before. The paper said

Coming Soon to the Biltmore Theater
Katherine Dunham and Her Dancers
in
Tropical Revue

Alvin looked carefully at the picture of Katherine Dunham, a beautiful dancer fluttering exotic ruffles. Katherine Dunham and her dance troupe were one of the few traveling shows in the world with black dancers performing dances from Africa, Haiti, and Latin America.

Alvin was curious. As he tucked the announcement into his pocket, he noticed Ted Crumb, a skinny boy with spindly legs, hanging out at a stage door nearby.

Ted knew all kinds of things about dance; he hoped to dance onstage someday. Ted told Alvin that Katherine Dunham's afternoon show was about to start and that they could see dancing like they'd never seen before.

Alvin and Ted crept down the alley that led to the Biltmore's stage entrance. They kept quiet and out of sight. With the stage door opened just so, they watched the splendor of *Tropical Revue*.

Katherine Dunham and her dancers swirled and lunged to the rhythms of West Indian drums. They were famous for *Bahiana,* a spicy Brazilian routine, and for a sizzling number called *Rumba with a Little Jive Mixed In.* Alvin's soul danced along when he saw Katherine Dunham's style.

Alvin nudged Ted. "What is that they're doing? What *is* that?" he asked.

"That's modern dancing," Ted said. "Watch this!"

Ted tried Katherine Dunham's *Bahiana*. Alvin slapped out a beat on his knees and followed Ted's lead.

Slowly, Alvin began to move. He curled his shoulders from back to front and rippled his hands like an ocean wave. He rolled his hips in an easy, steady swivel, dancing with an expression all his own.

Alvin moved like a cat, *smooth* like quicksilver. When he danced, happiness glowed warm inside him.

Dusk crept over the city. The streetlights of Central Avenue winked on, one by one. Alvin made his way back to East 43rd Place.

That night, Alvin told his mother he'd seen black people performing their own special dances. It was a show Alvin would never forget.

1949–1953
Lester Horton's Dance School

More than anything, Alvin wanted to study dance. But when Alvin arrived in Los Angeles not everyone could take dance lessons. In 1949 not many dance schools accepted black students. And almost none taught the fluid moves that Alvin liked so much — almost none but the Lester Horton Dance Theater School, a modern dance school that welcomed students of all races.

Lester's door was open to anyone serious about learning to dance. And, at age eighteen, Alvin Ailey was serious, especially when he saw how Lester's dancers moved. One student, Carmen de Lavallade, danced with a butterfly's grace. Another, James Truitte, made modern dance look easy. But Lester worked his students hard. Sometimes they danced all day.

After hours in the studio, droplets of sweat dotted Alvin's forehead. He tingled inside, ready to try Lester's steps once more. At first, Alvin kept time to Lester's beat and followed Lester's moves. Then Alvin's own rhythm took over, and he started creating his own steps. Alvin's tempo worked from his belly to his elbows, then oozed through his thighs and feet.

"What is Alvin *doing*?" one student asked.

"Whatever he's doing, he's sure doing it fine," two dancers agreed.

Some tried to follow Alvin's moves, but even Alvin didn't know which way his body would reel him next.

Alvin's steps flowed from one to another. His loops and spins just came to him, the way daydreams do.

Alvin danced at Lester Horton's school almost every day. He taught the other students his special moves.

In 1950, Alvin joined Lester Horton's dance company. Soon Alvin performed his own choreography for small audiences who gathered at Lester's studio. Alvin's dances told stories. He flung his arms and shim-shammed his middle to express jubilation. His dips and slides could even show anger and pain. Modern dance let Alvin's imagination whirl.

All the while, Lester watched Alvin grow into a strong dancer and choreographer. Lester told Alvin to study and learn as much as he could about dance. He encouraged Alvin to use his memories and his African-American heritage to make dances that were unforgettable.

1958–1960
Blues Suite–Revelations

Alvin's satchel hung heavy on his shoulder. His shoes rapped a beat on the sidewalk while taxicabs honked their horns. He was glad to be in New York City, where he came to learn ballet from Karel Shook and modern dance techniques from Martha Graham, two of the best teachers in the world.

Alvin took dance classes all over town, and he met dancers who showed him moves he'd never seen before. So many dancers were black. Like Alvin, their dreams soared higher than New York's tallest skyscrapers.

Alvin gathered some of the dancers he'd seen in classes around the city. He chose the men and women who had just the right moves to dance his choreography. Alvin told them he wanted to start a modern dance company that would dance to blues and gospel music — the heritage of African-American people. Nine dancers believed in Alvin's idea. This was the beginning of the Alvin Ailey American Dance Theater.

On March 30, 1958, on an old wooden stage at the 92nd Street Y, Alvin and his friends premiered with *Blues Suite*, dances set in a honky-tonk dance hall. Stage lights cast moody shadows against the glimmer of each dancer's skin. The women flaunted red-hot dresses with shoes and stockings to match; the men wore black hats slouched low on their heads. They danced to the swanky-swank of a jazz rhapsody.

Alvin's choreography depicted the blues, that weepy sadness all folks feel now and then. *Blues Suite* stirred every soul in the room.

Alvin was on his way to making it big. Word spread quickly about him and his dancers. Newspapers hailed Alvin. Radio stations announced his debut.

An even bigger thrill came when the 92nd Street Y asked Alvin to perform again. He knew they hardly ever invited dance companies to come back. Alvin was eager to show off his next work.

On January 31, 1960, gospel harmonies filled the concert hall at the 92nd Street Y.

Rock-rock-rock
Rocka-my-soul
Ohhh, rocka-my-soul

Alvin clapped in time to the music, the same way he did when he was a boy. But now, Alvin rejoiced onstage in *Revelations,* a suite of dances he created to celebrate the traditions of True Vine Baptist Church in Navasota, Texas.

The audience swayed in their seats as Alvin and his company gloried in their dance. High-stepping ladies appeared onstage sweeping their skirts. They danced with grace and haughty attitudes. Alvin and the other men jumped lively to the rhythm, strutting and dipping in sassy revelry.

Revelations honored the heart and the dignity of black people while showing that hope and joy are for everyone. With his sleek moves, Alvin shared his experiences and his dreams in a way no dancer had ever done.

When *Revelations* ended, the audience went wild with applause. They stomped and shouted. "More!" they yelled. *"More!"*

Taking a bow, Alvin let out a breath. He raised his eyes toward heaven, satisfied and proud.

Alvin Ailey, January 1979, © Jack Mitchell

By exploring the African-American cultural experience through dance, Alvin Ailey changed the face of American dance forever. The Alvin Ailey American Dance Theater (AAADT) was one of the first integrated American dance companies to gain international fame. Two years after the creation of *Revelations*, Mr. Ailey's company performed in the Far East, Southeast Asia, and Australia on a tour sponsored by the U.S. State Department. Since Mr. Ailey founded his company in 1958, it has performed for an estimated 15 million people in forty-eight states, forty-five countries, and on six continents.

In 1965, Mr. Ailey met Judith Jamison, a vibrant young dancer whose talent and energy inspired him to create *Cry*, a piece that honors the struggles and triumphs of black women. That 1971 work is now a popular Alvin Ailey classic.

Mr. Ailey was born in Rogers, Texas, on January 5, 1931. During his life, Mr. Ailey received many honors. In 1982, he received the United Nations Peace Medal. He was awarded the Kennedy Center Honor and the Handel Medallion in December 1988. Mr. Ailey died on December 1, 1989, in New York City.

Today, under the direction of Ms. Jamison, the Alvin Ailey American Dance Theater still mesmerizes audiences everywhere. Mr. Ailey's dance tradition continues at the Alvin Ailey American Dance Center—an accredited dance academy in New York City—where boys and girls study ballet, modern dance, and tap dance. The Alvin Ailey Repertory Ensemble, the resident company of the school, is a troupe of young dancers who perform throughout the United States.

"This is a book that could have been illustrated in a number of different ways, but it is hard to imagine any art that would have been more handsome than the pictures provided by Colón. . . . The illustrations glow with a warmth that shows what makes holidays special." —Booklist

Celebration!

By Jane Resh Thomas · Illustrated by Raul Colón

From where Maggie sits on the front steps, she can see both ways up and down the street. Her feet jiggle, as if they won't hold still. She spots the old car when it turns the corner. It jerks like a balky horse because Granny still hasn't learned how to drive very well since Grandpa had his stroke and landed in the nursing home.

"Picnic time!" Maggie yells into the house to Mom and Pop. "Here comes Granny!"

By the time Granny pulls up at the curb, Pop and Mom and Maggie are all lined up, while Shadow the dog prances between their legs. He gives Maggie a big slurp across her cheek. Shadow loves good times as much as anybody.

"Am I the first one here?" says Granny.

"You're always the first one here, whether it's the Fourth of July or not," says Pop with his booming laugh. "You always come an hour early. We'd be disappointed if you didn't!"

He helps when Granny's hair net snags on the edge of the door. Mom hugs her and takes the plate with Granny's famous chocolate cake. Pop hoists the gallon jugs of her special lemonade with rings of lemon floating on the top, one jug on each hip. Granny hands Maggie a jar of homemade pickles. Maggie's mouth is watering, set for all of her favorite foods, even though she ate a peanut butter sandwich ten minutes ago to keep from starving to death.

And here come Uncle Jake and Aunt Alberta in their station wagon.

"Thank goodness everybody's early," says Maggie. "I couldn't wait for the party to start." She puts her hand flat on the car window, covering the hand of her cousin Ann on the other side of the glass. Ann and Arthur and Abbie and Alice and Little Jake pile through the back doors, so excited they're practically crawling over each other.

"We brought our jump rope," says Ann.

"Carry your share of the food to the refrigerator," Aunt Alberta says, "then play." She doles out a dish of food to each of her kids. Maggie sees baked beans, macaroni salad, and pork chops under the plastic wrap.

Now Arthur and Little Jake are in the brand-new pool Mom and Dad just built. Abbie and Alice swing the rope on the back walk while Ann and Maggie jump, holding hands, alongside the picnic table Pop made out of boards laid across sawhorses. Maggie feels like Ann's sister, maybe even her twin; they jump in perfect unity.

The grown-ups all sit together in the rickety lawn chairs, but Maggie notices that nobody takes the place where Grandpa used to sit, nearest the big maple tree.

"Howdy," calls Pop.

"Hi there," Mom says to the neighbors on both sides whose families have gathered for their own picnics.

Shadow climbs as far into Granny's lap as a big dog can get and licks her neck. "Some watchdog you are," she says. "If the burglars come here some dark night, you'll get 'em down and lick 'em to death."

"Whoop!" says Pop. "Here's Charlie."

And up the alley, here comes that silver car Uncle Charlie and Aunt Aretha bought to celebrate when they finished law school. Uncle Charlie parks it very carefully by the garage, in the shade of the lilac bushes.

"Here comes the law!" Uncle Jake calls out. "How's everything at the courthouse?"

"Pretty good." Uncle Charlie adjusts his glasses and brushes at his Bermuda shorts. Aunt Aretha hands Mom a big bowl of raw vegetables and another one of dip.

Maurice—who wants to be called Michael, after Michael Jordan—trails along behind his folks with his face screwed up and sparks behind his eyes. At Christmas, he told Maggie he was too old for family stuff. She can see he didn't want to come. Will she be too old for Fourth of July, Maggie wonders, when she's thirteen like Maurice?

"I'm especially glad to see you, Michael," Mom says to him. "I've been warming up the basketball for a little one-on-one after the hot dogs."

Last night Maggie heard Mom whispering to Pop. "Pay special attention to Maurice tomorrow," she said. "Aretha's got him on a short leash because he pilfered some candy at the drugstore. She took him to the manager. Made him pay from his allowance and apologize."

Maggie studies her cousin's face to see whether shame shows through. She thinks of the times when she was tempted to steal. Thank goodness nobody knows; thank goodness nobody's whispering about her and some short leash! Maurice's boredom, she decides, is his way to hide every other feeling.

Uncle Charlie pokes the bottles of water he brought into the washtub filled with ice, among the cans of cola and ginger ale and the brown bottles of beer.

"Fancy bottled water, no better than out of the tap," mutters Pop, "but that's what Aretha and Charlie got to have." He sets up more lawn chairs for the newcomers, but Maurice wanders away to stand alone, leaning against the house.

Arthur and Little Jake are splashing each other in the pool, and the girls have jumped the rope a hundred and forty-eight times in a row without falling down. Now Maggie misses a beat and sprawls at Granny's feet. Shadow licks Maggie under her chin until she can't get up for giggles.

And here comes Aunt Lou, still dressed in her nurse's uniform, carrying pans of food and a beach bag and followed by her six kids.

"You look like a broody old hen," Pop calls from the barbecue, where he's trying to get the fire lit, "trailing all those chicks behind you."

Aunt Lou passes the pans off to Mom. "Vietnamese chicken wings," she says. Aunt Lou takes pride in her cooking.

"I have to test it," says Maggie. She dips her finger into the juice and licks it. "Umm," she says, ducking Lou's affectionate swat. "Aunt Lou, you're the best."

Everybody gathers around Lou as if she were a honeycomb and they were bees, all jabbering at once so nobody can hear what anybody's saying. Lou's kids burst out between the grown-ups' legs. Sally's got a Frisbee. James has brought the Hula Hoop he found in Granny's attic, from the time when Aunt Lou and Mom were girls.

A squirt gun sticks out of Leo's pocket, under his hand, where Lou can't see it. Kenny's shuffling his pack of cards; he's always practicing because he's going to be a magician and a tap dancer when he grows up. Asia has her best brown doll cradled in her arm; she's going to be a mommy. Willie's just dragging his blanket along behind him on the ground, sucking his thumb. His diapers look heavy, down around his knees.

"Best-behaved kids I ever saw," calls Pop from his place by the barbecue. "Unless it's Jake and Alberta's kids. Or Maurice. Or my own Maggie, here." He throws a wink at her.

Now Abbie and Alice and Ann and Maggie, Sally and James and Leo, and Kenny and Asia and Willie join the splashing at the pool. Maurice, alias Michael, who didn't want to come, walks up to the pool in his Chicago Bulls shirt and shorts.

"Stand aside," he says. He turns around and falls right over on his back into the water.

A wave hits Maggie in the face. "It's a tidal wave," she yells, and falls backward beside Maurice. They both come up with water streaming from their hair, giggling just like the little kids.

And here comes Uncle Frank, Mom's bachelor brother, the master of ceremonies, the bringer of fun, around the side of the house.

"Late as usual," says Granny.

"Let's put the hot dogs on the fire and give him some food before he drinks any beer," says Mom.

Maggie helps her spread bedsheets on the table and pins the corners down with rocks, in case the wind comes up. Aunt Lou's Vietnamese chicken wings are the centerpiece.

"Stick to drinking lemonade," says Granny, handing her youngest son a glass.

"Hey there, Frank," says Pop. "Have yourself a seat while I burn us some dogs!"

Maggie hugs her favorite uncle. "Did you bring 'em?" she says. "You didn't forget?"

Frank pats the long, narrow boxes in his hip pocket. "Do I ever forget?" he says. "Here's the fun, after the sun goes down. Sparklers!" He fans the boxes on the back of his hand.

"You kids dry off now." Aunt Lou tosses them the beach towels she brought in her bag and trails Mom, Granny, Alberta, and Aretha into the house. In a minute the door slams, and they all march back in a line carrying the food, as if they were delivering it on pillows to the king. They arrange the feast all up and down the table.

While Pop tends the hot dogs on the grill, Maggie snakes her hand out behind him and grabs an uncooked wiener, half for herself and half for Shadow.

"Maggie, I'm watching you with the eyes in the back of my head," says Pop. "You know we can't afford dogs for the dog."

Pop flips the hot dogs onto a plate. "Bring up your chairs, everybody," he yells, "and dig in."

O hooray for sparklers and jump ropes. Hooray for chicken wings and potato salad. O joy for Granny's lemonade, with rings of lemon floating on the top. Hooray for Uncle Frank, who cuts the chocolate cake because he's the math teacher and knows how to divide things into twenty-two equal parts.

Hooray for families who make room for everybody at picnics on the Fourth of July!